Letters I Never Sent

(The 28 Version)

Words Unspoken, Yet Unbroken: Poems I should have said earlier

Jiya Doshi

To my Mom, for filling my 1-year-old brain with rhymes and songs to the point that we had at least three different stacks of CDs and vinyl to pick from for car rides. Also, for listening to me rant. All day.

To my Dad, for feeding my incurable book addiction and for being the first (and only) reader of my most chaotic first drafts – sorry and thank you in advance.

To all the people who inspired these poems, knowingly or otherwise.

Now all I feel is repent,

Because these are the letters

that I never sent.

Preface

What if?

Star-lidded eyes showed me dreams that would haunt me someday,

At what could've been if things never did change,

And if everything was right in place,

Would "today" exist this way?

As I sat brooding, my what-ifs leading me to dead-end streets,

At the possibilities of my impossible dreams coming to reality,

Wondering about 'forever' like it was a starry night sky,

And I was a speck of dust that made you fly.

That's a poem I wrote about all the 'what ifs' that kept haunting me throughout my life. And throughout my life, there were things I meant to say to people.

And most of the time, I couldn't.

So, I'd sit in my room, writing stories and poetry, leaving hints, hoping they would figure it out.

But they never knew.

Whether it was good or bad, whether it's an "I can't survive without you" or maybe just "Get out of my life."

And so many times, everyone else figured it out except the people it was meant for (because *eye roll* of course), and it was too late and I had regrets. Big ones.

The 'what ifs' haunted me. They were at my heels, chasing me down the dark streets of parallel universes I made up in my head and to the edge of the cliffs and precipices I hung my if-onlys from.

And then came the guilt.

If only I had done it.

If only they knew.

If only...

It's hard to say the right thing at the right time. It's pure luck sometimes. It’s accidental. Like a rare shooting star.

And I have this gnawing fear that years from now, I'd probably be 80, and as I would go through my diaries, I would regret not saying anything when I had the chance.

The words were at the tip of my tongue. The phone was an inch from my finger. All I had to do was dial a number. Send a message.

(At this point, even a carrier pigeon didn’t seem like a bad option.)

The words that follow in the pages are those I wanted to say, but I couldn't, because every time I tried to, there was a voice in my head telling me to shut up.

And I ALWAYS listened to it.

But no excuses this time.

I don't know if the people these poems are about will ever read them.

I don't know if they'll even know that the poems ahead are about them.

Maybe it's too late now for me, but you can still do it.

Maybe, twenty-eight years from now, you'd look back and cringe at these moments. But maybe, just maybe, twenty-eight years from now, you'd be glad you said it.

So here it is.

A few letters I never sent.

A few words I never spoke.

A few poems I wish I could've shared earlier.

And here’s the raw version you’ve never seen before. Because it’s the 28 version. And anything with that number has only always spelled the rawest, craziest, and wildest version of myself.

I CAN BE

I feel like a bird perched on the Eiffel Tower,

The view below me making me wanna fly up higher,

Plot twists and knife twists don't really matter,

I'm on my tiptoes, walking like a Barbie till I ended up here.

I see the lights and breathe in the chilly breeze over the coffee,

I turn right and paint Mona Lisa under the name of Da Vinci,

I had every glass painted until it became Notre Dame,

But I keep changing my name.

So, you can call me progress,
You can call me an artist,
I can be your poet,
Talking of the colors in your iris.

I can be your daydream,
Of the visions making you wanna sleep,
I can be that story,
That makes you wanna think of me.

I can be that poster,
You hang in your room,
I can be that laughter,
Drawing you out of the gloom.

I feel like a fairy sitting upon Big Ben,

Hearing it strike, and counting down to ten,

There are thieves hiding their faces, but I can see them,

I don't care about the gold, I love the mayhem.

I hide under the sleeves and cloaks of passersby,

Sitting in a hackney and driving out of town,

I see the rain splashing from a gray blotched sky,

If the weather's down, I promise to be around.

You can call my name in the shadows,

Or just murmur it in your mind,

You can call me on the telephone,

Or do one of our eye-to-eyes.

I can tune my heartbeat to sound like thunder,

Bury a body or be the alibi to your blunder,

I can make all the police surrender,

You can wear your masks as long as you smile under.

I can be that idea,

You chase down the street,

I can get you nostalgia,

Whenever you think about me.

P.S:

Still yours.

Even unsent.

love, j

TIMELESS

A map of stars,

A constellation of scars,

Caresses on callouses, gems on all my talismans,

An empty throne for a promising king.

Cupid shoots down arrows, I keep dodging till I'm done,

We play the game of hide and seek, all I do is run,

Right under plain sight,

You laugh like I'm a spark of daylight.

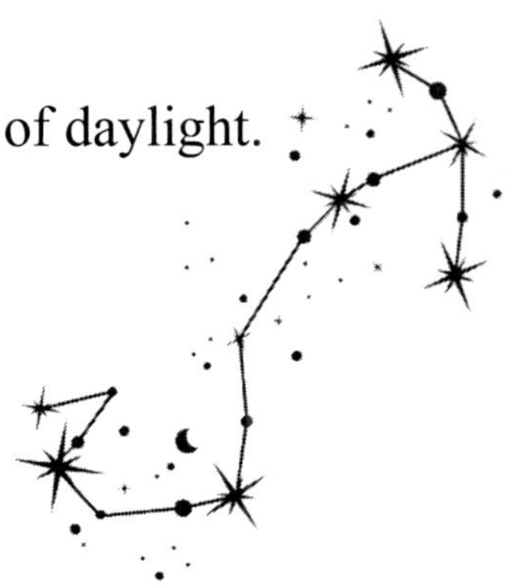

Dizziness stoops down on my porch till I stumble upon bright light,

Silhouettes under a dazzling night,

And all my sequin charms replace the hidden stars I locked,

Everything I brush feels like a static shock.

Search the smile you etched on my face,

Crack open that carapace,

Ferris wheels and candy bars, street lights and asphalt,

Waiting for us to come and halt.

Saturn keeps the rings to fling out at things,

Or change destinies, make parallel lines start meeting,

Pluto does the cheating, all the goddamn peeping,

But it really got me thinking.

Sunsets you painted, two moments before you fainted,

Into a world of dreams so bated,

I can see you waited, feet tapping, arms crossed,

You can see I hated, stuck in there, I felt lost.

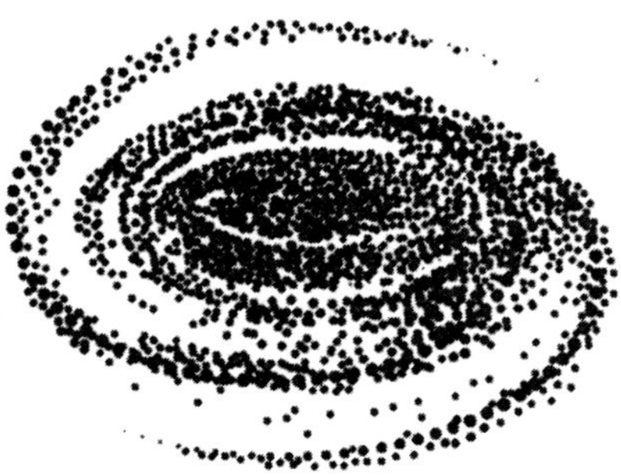

Counting the scenes till I forgot,

Fingers wriggling in distraught,

Sit by the shores, trace words in the sand,

Like they were lyrics, the waves my band.

Find the look in my eyes and hold it,

When I act like a goddamn idiot,

My words will be like the endless sea,

Uncontrollable, involuntary,

Blood and beat,

Timeless to see.

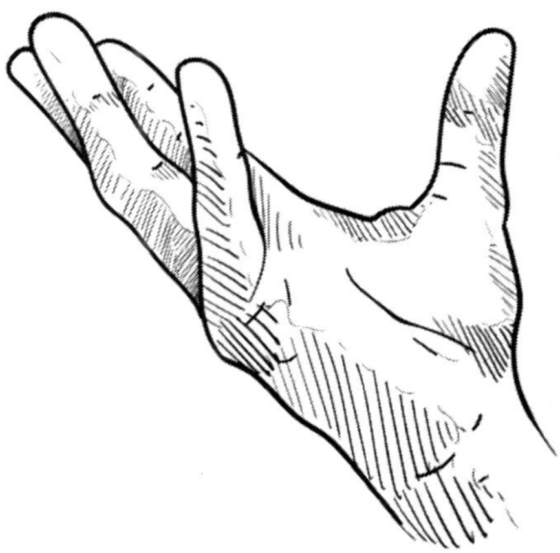

NEMESIS

Mosaics of gold, wisps of smoke,

Burning black under pretending,

I should have seen, I should've known,

But the light in my eyes was blinding.

Wrapped in wreaths of holly,

A poison unknown,

And you never said sorry,

You just left me on my own.

You entered like a star,

A dream that ended way before it started,

I reached out far enough to lose sight of my path,

To know the place you left your trails was a bait into the dark.

Spears of silver, I crumple to my knees,

The apple was poison right to the core,

Indelible marks etched into my skin,

You made me the fire that burns you to ashes forevermore.

The graffiti words sprayed on the walls,

Silver spun webs, broken crystals of fame,

Screams of silence, dried up falls,

Weakened frame, dusted name,

That was all I became, and that is all it was.

Cracked mirror, strangling vines,

I couldn't imagine anything worse than this,

I would've lost sight of all that was mine,

I wish I could've seen you earlier - seen you as my nemesis.

You think you can be a mirror - redirecting my shine,

But there's more to it than this,

I'll burn you down with time,

It's time you realize it, my dear nemesis,

There's a lot more to it than this.

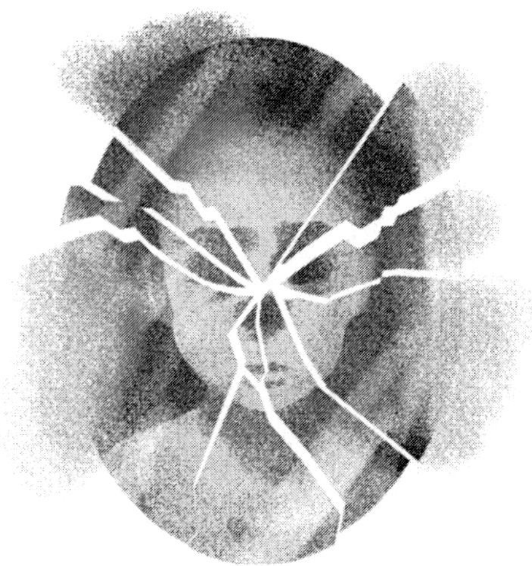

PASSING FRIENDS

It was a swish of fabrics, a wish to escape really quick,

I thought I saw a peek under the hood, a wish of so much that could,

Be, a graffiti on the street,

I'd go there every week.

It came pounding like a storm come true,

Stories of me and you,

Passing friends like passing trends,

Such things, you know, always end.

I was in a trance, all you cared about was the dance,

Heels clicking, the lights were blinking out,

Everyone was staring, and I didn't have the heart to tell you why,

So I let you walk away like a stranger I passed by.

Your gloss was the shade of metal grays and fuchsia,

You dressed to impress - I knew that so far,

You let your hair down, eyes like the double edge to this town,

You should've thought twice before you let me down.

It was a dirty dish I didn't wash, an empty party that was too gauche,

Like cutting myself and rubbing some salt,

Running across the wrong room screaming your name,

Prank calling and then everything changed,

Nothing was the same.

It came pounding like a storm come true,

Stories of me and you,

Passing friends like passing trends,

Such things, you know, always end.

Like being in free fall, trapped in a time loop,

Back when we had nicknames for me and you,

You had your reasons - you found your own people,

I didn't need another explanation for this.

First, you changed the way you talked,

Grew to follow, never to question the walk,

Then all we talked about was Pinterest,

Random pins and soon we lost interest...

...And ended up here,

It could've been more than just a few years,

More than talking about books,

Till I almost forgot about you,

After 20,000 fears and nightmares,

Tossing in bed, waking up in cold sweat,

And I was almost forgetting it all, forgetting you were still there,

Until today.

CARELESS

Broken light rays, refracted,

Sharpening knives that are rusted,

You see my words, not the way I acted,

My unspoken mirror speeches now dusted.

I found a scar that still hurts me,

A bed of rose thorns – look where that's got us,

Suffocating parking lots and the car keys,

They say we've gone rogue, but that's not really much,

There's no crime as long as there's us.

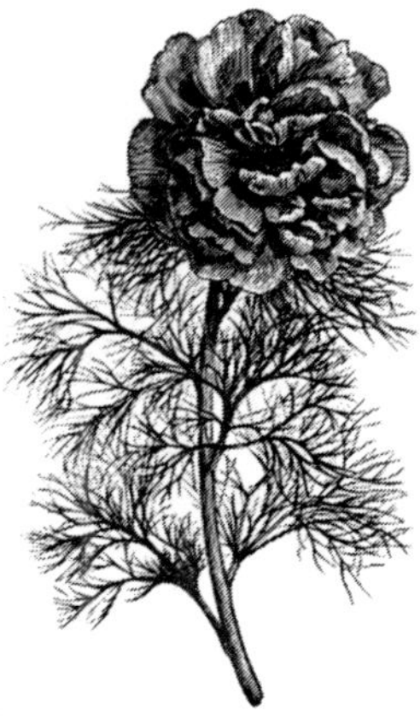

Spent all the cash on the vending machine, our pockets now empty,

Spent all our plans trying to fix things that didn't blow up,

I broke all the mirrors, but I still see me,

I still see what I've become.

You saved the last can for a real meal,

You raised a toast on an empty street,

You had a party, but there was only me,

But for the first time, I saw you happy,

Not just pretending to be.

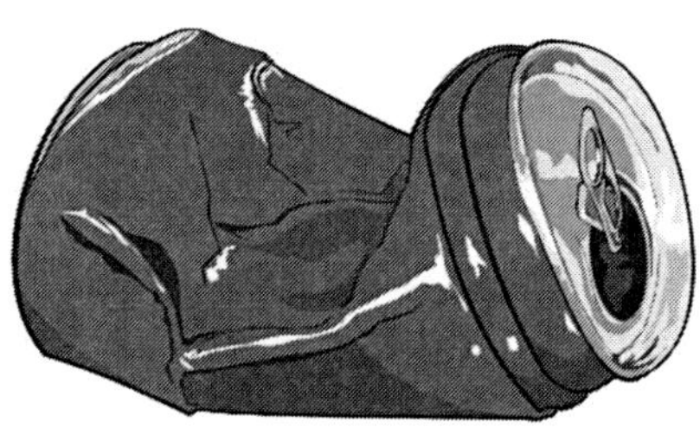

Hairpins pushed through keyholes, hidden secrets,

Quicksilver smile, vignette shadows,

You know I hate the yellow brick road, so I faked it,

And you trust it like the only thing you know.

I found a star after 101 sleepless nights,

Caught sight of flashlights from the car you stole,

No license, no risk, it's worth a try,

You know I'm only me when I'm alone,

With you on our carefree night.

'Cause this is gonna be a rare phenomenon,

Where I don't need to care about what they say or see me as,

Hooded tee and up-to-no-good.

You don't need to think ten moves ahead – we're not playing chess.

Reckless, like a sliver of moonlight that caught into your hair,

Fearless, like the shades of twilight,

Having no care.

P.S:

Is this a metaphor disguised as a memory, or a memory disguised as a poem? Either way, it was never meant to be sent.

STUCK AT TWILIGHT

The sky was my bulletin board, the stars my secret message,

My footsteps on the pavement, my hands shoved in my pockets,

I knew every constellation like the scars from thrusting my hands in the hedge,

And yet it was a stranger, forgotten not yet forgiven.

I dreamed of unexpected happenings blooming like rosebuds in my backyard,

I saw their thorns staining a perfectly dark heart to a shade of crimson red,

I watch as the ace lies flat on the table, a smirking devil card,

I shut my eyes, yet see all the broken mirrors lying ahead.

I snooped around the wrong tree at the wrong time,

Got my sneaker stuck in a fissure during my climb,

And it refuses to go back, go forth, stay on,

Writhing like a daisy in an uprooting storm.

I paint how its petals give away to an eddy of white,

Swirling through the winds in a perfect pas de deux,

And the last petal, clinging to some telephone booth in the night,

Falls as the “she loves me” petal on a despondent lover’s head, the cue to call, and say “I love you.”

And the daisy floats to my mind, stuck
between contradictions of derivatives,

Trying to make all my findings evidence,

My heart lurched, like I'd hit the brakes,

Reminding me of all my mistakes.

And maybe I was that daisy, being played
around by them all,

The quiet hush of the street, the hiss of a
lamplight blinking to life,

Maybe I was the spring they chose to call,

To bring back flowers in bouquets,
handwritten love letters, poems that rhyme.

Maybe I was a flightless bird who tried flying,

My eyes like the warm sunrise that hadn't begun yet,

My head was a kite that I let soar past midnight,

And I haven't forgiven half the things I forget,

Made familiarity a stranger to my senses,

Like it would help me stay on the fences...

But maybe I wasn't meant to stay,

I was meant to echo like the moon on thousands of broken shards of glass,

Its moonlight refracting and forming a rainbow through the curtain,

Sending a message no one thought could ever pass.

Back when I didn't know the right side over the easy,

Just before I let myself be the sky the sea would be reflecting,

I didn't know I'd end up pallid from the plummet into me,

Time an endless loop I wish would stop repeating.

Maybe Doctor Strange had it right all along,

Maybe my present was a loop, maybe I was stuck in time,

Blind to the night breaking into dawn,

Because I thrived at the blend of it all, I thrived only in twilight.

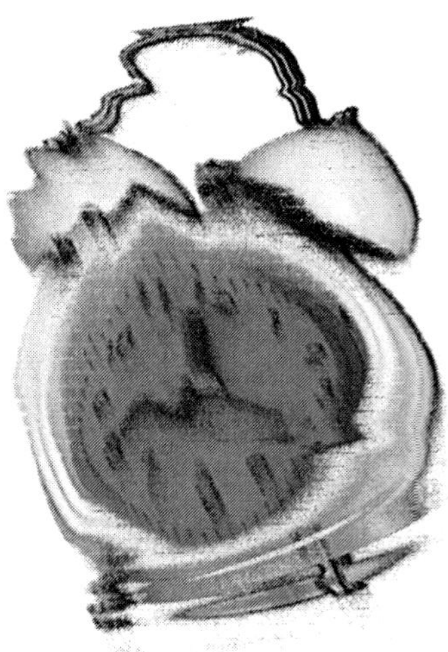

I'm just stuck at twilight,

Flushed cheeks from a fever, my hands shoved in the pockets,

The stars are my message, the beachscape my highlight,

The midnight beat me black and blue, my blood dawned crimson and scarlet,

As the meteors shot like rockets I'd once dreamed to fly.

So go on, be the contrast to my contradiction,

Be the poet to my poem, try,

I'm the Icarus to your ocean,

Go on and be the reason, the reason why…

I'm just stuck at twilight,

Trying to go back, go forth, stay on,

Wincing at the sight, almost stupefied,

Like a daisy blown away in the storm…

Just stuck at twilight,

Stuck at twilight.

IT'S MINE!

Western coast, winter equinox, I'm playing hide and seek with the waves,

Splashing it in my face, hoping I'd wake up from this place,

Back in my bedroom, staring at the ceiling, wisps of a haze,

Crawling over the third quarter faze,

Of the moon screaming it's nearly complete,

Telling me this is the very day,

You finally made it.

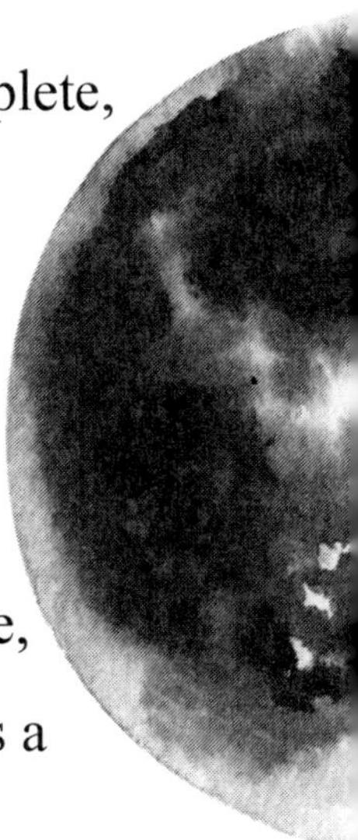

And then on the spring equinox,

I saw something I couldn't quite believe,

Until I tested it with a punch like it was a faulty torch,

Which I needed to hit before it finally lit,

And here I was on the hunt for peace,

Ending up in, well, pieces.

The syllables I'd spoken,

Had only ever been uttered by myself,

And on your voice, it sounds so broken,

'Cause it was never meant for anyone else.

Shh, it's a secret,

Between me and the walls of my mind,

It's for my ears only – how did you hear it?

How did you steal it from inside?

Someday you'd see the good in goodbye,

When you finally look it in the eye,

You'll know that this is just meant to be mine,

Today, tomorrow, and all the time.

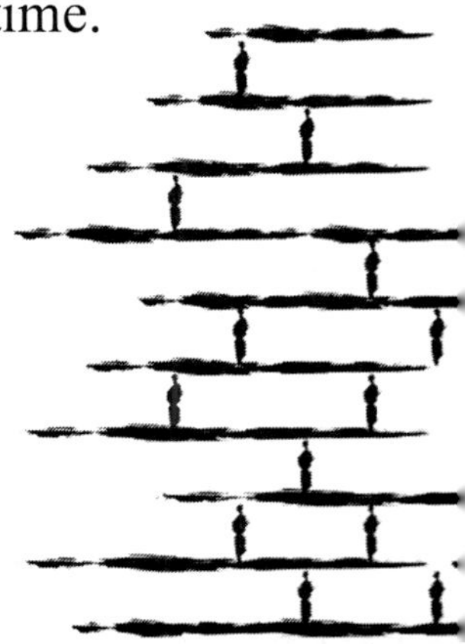

You snatched it like a flying scarf in the air,

Beginner's luck in your pocket,

But my very existence had the air,

You hit a sixer, the audience applauded,

And I stood in a corner, as you got it,

Instead.

The first time that I heard it,

I thought I heard my own name,

And I smiled at the thought that history repeated,

That things really didn't change.

But then I realized it was your name, not mine,

It sounded so wrong, I laughed and cried at myself,

I splashed the water in my face, salt stinging my eyes,

'Cause probably I needed it so that no one could tell,

How my senses flashed out like a 70s TV out of signal,

Glitching like a projection, feeling unreal.

Shh, it's a secret,

Between me and the walls of my mind,

It's for my ears only – how did you hear it?

How did you steal it from inside?

When you know it's mine.

SOMEDAY

People meet, and people depart,
But they will always stay in the heart;
Despite the distance, despite the heat,
Someday we will surely meet.

Turns out life twisted our paths away,
Can't go back to see where it did,
Because moments gone are memories today,
And all I can do is relive.

Someday it'll reach out to you again,
Someday I'll find your trail,
It may be hidden, slightly faint,
But I'll see it through both mud and rain.

I'll leave behind,

A piece of me,

For you to find,

Without which I'll never be complete.

The autumn leaves will fall,

The melted snow starts to crawl;

The spring blooms will grow and wither away,

But what matters is today.

Our paths lay scattered away,

Like dandelion seeds flying far,

And every night we wish just the same,

As we look upon shooting stars.

The honeysuckles have grown sparse,

Its scent is no comfort,

We've gone too far,

To return.

But there's more to this fairytale,

Than what it says,

Our paths will cross, our ways,

Will see the same flowers someday.

DAYDREAM

You had the onyx fit into the ceiling for me,
And silver sparkles as the stars,
I was transported into a daydream,
But I knew it'd end way before it started,
Last as far as I've been thinking,
And yet I couldn't help sinking,
With it.

I treated the pen and paper on the desk like,
It was a phone in my hands and,
I could feel my face under the light,
The lamp casting shadows and highlights,
Even if it was from a painting,
I knew it was just what I'd been wanting,
All this time.

And the pale rays of the moon,
Cascaded right into my room,
I could almost feel the shores,
So close I could control it,
Even when it would be miles from home.

I treated the ink on my fingers,
As a shadow ring I'd created,
Spinning gold yarns into jars,
That I'd store throughout the winter,
And the sand in the hourglass kept dripping by,
Years of things I couldn't pass by,

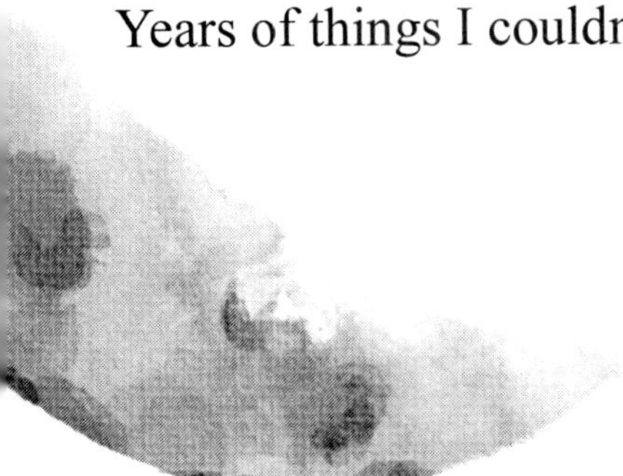

Daydreams and reality formed into words,
As I watched the stories unfurl.
Raven sky, invisible clouds,
Soundless footsteps on the asphalt,
Muffed by the layers of snow,
And I sat staring through the window.

The candle flame flared up like a star,
And I say let's go as far,
As the moon rays have dared to reach,
And let's cross those horizons,
Show them that we're wild and free,
Even if it is just in a daydream,
I'd make it to be a masterpiece,
Some way you could remember me.

And maybe someday I would be buried in a grave of words,

And return here as a flock of birds,

Or a ghost roaming about the land,

Reaching out to you with empty hands.

And I would flash like a shooting star you would wish upon,

Cursing in the dark, I'd make it all come true till you forgot who I was,

Just a tale of light,

A phoenix in flight,

Burning just for you,

A forgotten locket from the ashes, the sparks that flew,

Just a bit of something that would make you dream,

About me.

Dust on the piano keys,

Typewriter jammed and useless without me,

And if I cannot write you a song, I'd sing it as the wind through your curtain,

Pluck you from the crossroads, certain,

As long as I could make you daydream,

About me.

THAT ONE FRIEND

White lies on the shore and the sand,

I was pale in the face, and you saw it alright,

X and O's drawn on my hand,

That's how it all started for the very first
time.

I wanted to lie, but you already knew,

We were bored sick when we first met eyes,

If I were a flame, I'd be burning blue,

I read you like my favorite story book, and it
felt like...

I was seeing through a mirror,

Hints of reflection and a whole world
beyond,

A mahogany table we were singing across,

I knew all that was going on.

Cracks appeared through that mask of yours,

Flames leapt off my eyes right onto the wood,

When I saw you for what you truly are,

That's when I really understood.

Writing gibberish and arguing which is more,

An army of poltergeists and phantom calls,

A magazine of modern monsters from folklore,

A bunch of characters making no sense at all.

Those flames toppled over like an array of dominoes,

A haze settled over, wrapping it like a present,

It was washed ashore,

The day we became friends.

DEAR YOU

The sun rays on my face,

Like the days I can never forget,

You turned the slightest spark into a blaze,

And this is the specialty of how special I felt.

I'd written endless speeches I never had the nerve to say,

Letters simply lying on my desk,

Yellowed pages, like withered flowers on a grave,

All of them, just lying unsent.

But there was this one which I wished I had read earlier,

'Cause if you'd never see, you wouldn't know my regret,

I wish this would stop feeling like forever,

This way isn't my way of choosing some other choice instead.

What was there yesterday won't remain,

Forever exists only in dreams,

At times, tomorrow becomes too late,

So I'd always be there whenever you need me.

I'm sorry for the fire,

I blame myself for it every second,

Wanna stop making myself feel like a liar,

Let's just stop the pretense of the of the pretense of ignorance.

It feels like every statue of the weeping angels has my face,

Feeling like I was Atlas holding up the entire sky,

So I write this to you today,

This is the first time I'd like to reverse time,

Make things alright,

Find my peace of mind.

I'm done exchanging secret glances,

When you don't know what I mean by them,

My pen is shaking, but I'm taking my chances,

If change begins, I'd like to be the one starting them.

I try to show how sorry I am, but it just seems so wrong,

I wish you knew I can never forget,

The million drafts in my inbox each 5 feet long,

And these letters, which I could never send.

All addressed to you, yet sent only when I'm dreaming,

So Dear You, I hope you never read this,

I guess it's too late, and it's lost all its meaning,

But please don't hate me, even though I would not blame you for it.

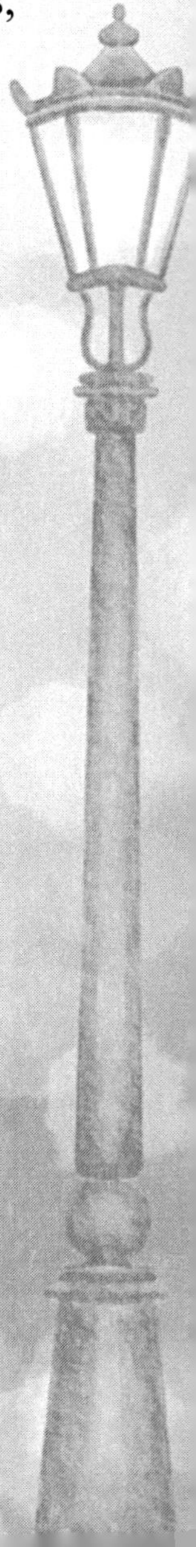

THIS WAY

You made a map of my scars like they were
a pretty thing,

Rocks studded with diamonds from some
century old meteorite,

Sounds of the laughter, the groans of the
swing,

Grass blades lit with dew like molten faerie
lights.

The scraping wood and scrabble boards,

Hushed whispers through the keyholes,

A coffee-drained vending machine on the
way home,

Chainmail over the last hope.

A kingdom of nothing, a queen with no crown,

You have the gun aimed, but can't pull the trigger,

It's a strategy game, my cards are all laid down,

I let you win, even if it makes me surrender.

'Cause I've never felt this way before,

Flashback to the blood rush, flashforward to the secret smile,

To the petrichor and sounds of a forevermore,

No one knows what it feels like…

Hands in the pocket, casually walking,

The sunset has never looked this way before,

I had my guard up, now I don't know what I was guarding,

Each star gets me hoping, but I don't know what I'm wishing for.

The scene was like it was picked out from a polaroid,

Drenched in photo frames, they're all trapped in pages now,

Shattered like a maelstrom, blowing dandelions across the void,

Brought together like a present, got rid of the 'what ifs' and 'hows'.

You cursed my name three times, then stuck out a hand,

Rolled your eyes and then came up with a plan,

I grabbed onto it like a quick tide, even though it was mad,

Partied like a fool, made the li lest things grand.

Driving in circles across the asphalt road,

Smoke drifting in the sparse light like we did on the first night,

Headlights aglow, no one turned up for the show,

Heatwaves from the tires creeping out of sight.

A city of gold, a king with everything,

I had the upper hand, I had the matches,

There seemed no going back, I knew what I was risking,

But lighting them would turn me too to ashes.

'Cause you've never felt this way before,

Flashback to the first laugh, flashforward to the letters,

To the bouquets of roses and sounds of a forevermore,

I've never felt safer, fingers coiled around the phone, I've never felt better,

I've never felt this way before.

P.S.

And sometimes fiction has a way of inspiring reality – and vice versa.

EVER AFTERS

I really don't wanna be the sad song you sing on the way home,

Driving on the highway all alone,

I wish I could be the happy endings I read about when I was four,

Years after you stopped believing in them anymore.

I know you hate happily ever afters,

Cut open my heart, and I'd tell you each one,

Now I'm on the train all alone, hearing distant laughter,

Of two kids having fun, right before one grew up.

Why do you wanna wake with the cobwebs of tears?

Remember how we sang songs together?

I'd try and find the verses with hands trembling with fears,

And we'd be talking of what happens next – the ever afters.

Now I'm crying in my room,

Throwing stones to some other moon,

Calling your name in the gloom,

But it was too soon.

I really don’t wanna be the shaky breath when you hear the radio,

Jaw set and driving on,

Your knuckles white from holding the steering wheel too hard so,

You focus your eyes on what is gone.

I know you hate happily ever afters,

Creep up to me like when we were kids – I’d have a book,

Now I stare at the ceiling, hearing the distant laughter,

Your unbelieving face when I talked about ‘happy’ to you.

Why do you wanna wake up in cold sweat?

Nightmare after nightmare,

Sing sad songs and start to regret,

Believe in anything at all when,

You're always left on the same street, same rain, same pain, again.

Now I'm dreaming in my room,

Reading fairytales like when I was two,

Throwing stones to some other you,

Who'd say you'd believe it too.

You know I love happily ever afters,

Drunk on it like a mad storyteller,

You know I love the sound of laughter –
thrown stones hitting the water,

Believing in forever,

A poet like no other,

Believing in happily ever afters.

FREE TO GO NOW

You're free to go now,

From my sight, from my dreams,

Haunting me up all night,

Do you know what it's all about?

No, because you can't see,

The way I cried.

You're free to go now,

'Cause the very last time I'd ever meet your eye,

Was when I was sweeter than nice,

Knowing I'd never see you, never knew you'd come back around,

Like a little white lie,

Tucked underneath your tie.

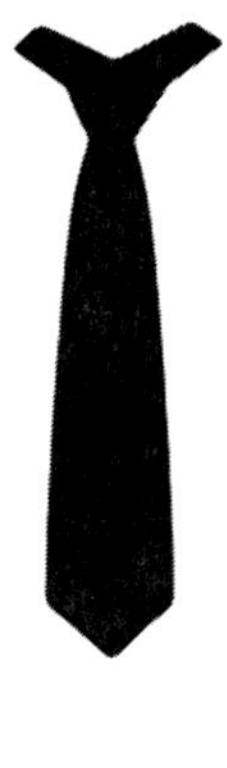

You’re free to go now,

‘Cause my lips hurt from wearing a smile,

You tell me I’m pretty when I wear my hair loose,

I try and try to act so low down,

No one sees the fire in my eyes,

But you do, you do.

You’re free to go now,

Free to leave my life like you left me on the street,

Took all my friends like they were a trophy,

Then acted so nice how,

Do you switch your masks? Please,

Tell me, please tell me.

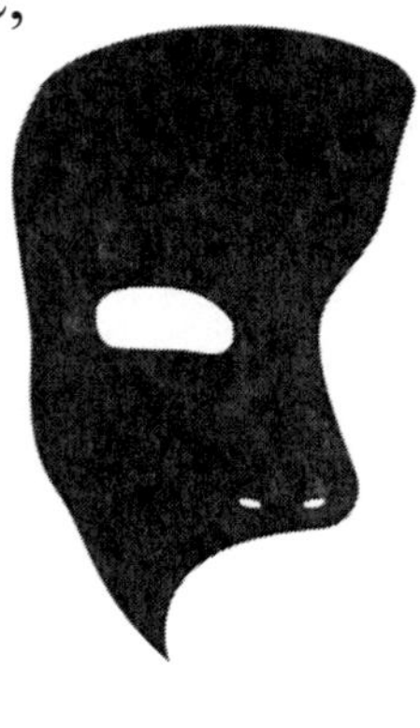

You're free to go now,

And leave me on my own,

'Cause finally I thought I'd never see you,

But then you come back around,

And rubbed it in my wounds,

Till I hit the door.

You gotta go now,

I got my hands full,

But if it's you versus me once more,

I promise I'll make you pay now,

Make you cry like I do after every dream so null, everything so dull,

I promise you more now, I promise you more.

You gotta go now,

Stop acting like a fool,

I wore my brocade robes,

That lit up my face in a way how,

It used to be before you,

Before you made me feel like a fault, like
I'm broke.

You're free to go now,

You stalked me like I was on a reality TV
show,

And you were the host,

That loved my gossip over her cold tea how,

You smirked when you saw me cold,

And told everyone you knew of.

But you gotta go now,

Leave behind the show now,

The way you made me feel like an outlaw,

Then drenched me like the rain how,

My tears seep through the pages how,

I felt when I first saw…

You gotta go before I should,

Tell them of the glint in your eyes of no good,

The cold little heart that I took,

The black veins of jealous shook,

'Cause they saw someone that should,

Have beaten you left, right, and center in school.

You're free to go now,

From my sight, from my dreams,

Haunting me up all night,

Do you know what it's all about?

No, because you can't see,

The way I cried when you stole what was mine.

CITYSCAPE

Should I write down a letter,

Handwritten and passed under the desk?

And you know me for the better,

Understand me like no one else.

When I'm running like a bullet shot through the air,

You're like the thunder crashing on a still lake,

All the corridors hushed like they're all holding their breath,

We're kicking the dirt, running down the railings, fingers trailing down the stairs.

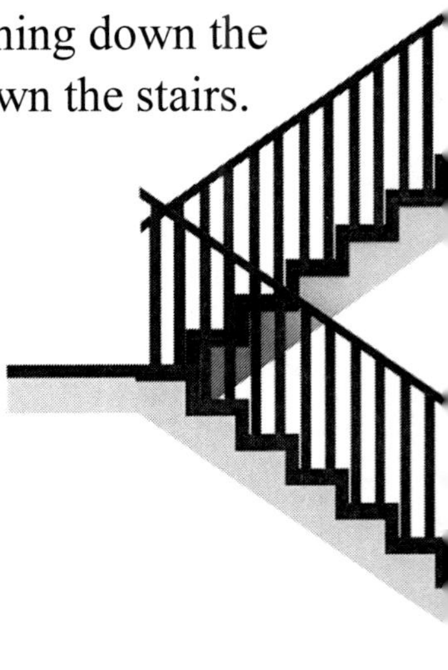

We're painting the cityscape in shades and shadows,

Leaping skyscrapers in the moonlight,

Sunset hues on my hoodie, twilight on the door,

I'm thinking of the dawn break after tonight.

Could I fake a party,

Invitation and cursive fonts?

'Cause I could be,

The host and the ghost whom you haunt.

Jumping like a spring wound up in coils,

I'm like the rough waves during high tide,

You sense it, all the streets are dead-ends, robberies are foiled,

And we're grinning away, unguarded, hiding nothing inside.

We’re painting the cityscape in shades and shadows,

Leaping skyscrapers, counting stars on fingers,

Sunset hues on my hoodie, twilight on the door,

I’m thinking of the changes, you think of what lingers.

So here's to you, here's to the laugh,

Here's to our fights, 12am calls,

I know I’m not right, but I know I’m not wrong,

Chasing the shadows, ending up with the storms.

Two thieves in the dark,

Dragged to the light,

And when we’re caught,

In the crime:

Pickpocketing the other, now we both got nothing,

The gun’s out of bullets, we run like criminals,

Get onto a train and leave the town to its ruins.

We're painting the cityscape in shades and shadows,

Trying to bring the loose ends together,

Sunset hues on my hoodie, twilight on the door,

And we call this our forever.

Shall I tell you a plot twist,

Spoil the fun of the ending?

I had the knife never used it,

And that's saying something.

All the roses were a bunch of thorns,

We're part of the go-getter, finders-keepers lot,

And before thoughts even take form,

We hit the bull's eye right on the spot.

Trying to figure out silhouettes,

Sticking to the shadows of the lamppost, knowing traps are laid,

Roaming around like we couldn't care less,

'Cause we were the ones who built this cityscape,

Set it to fire,

Brought it to life,

But this is our place, we do what we like.

P.S.

It was ours to rule, and it was ours to destroy.

LOST AND FOUND

I'm done writing pages,

Take me out of my cages,

I sit with the keys,

To my old diary,

My scrawls become poetry,

My mindless musings my stories.

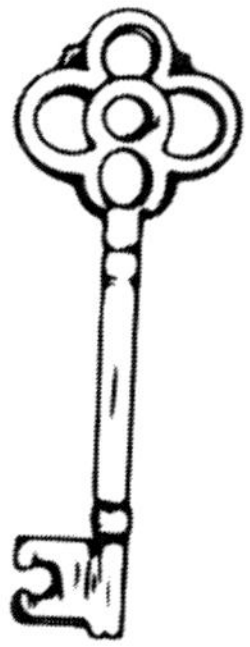

Was it a bullet that cut through the air,

When I was talking and walking down the stairs?

Was it a dagger I should've sensed and caught in my palm?

I should've covered my sleeves with my heart, but it hit my arm.

I am lying in a pile of lost and found,

Waiting for you to come around,

Sitting cross-legged, borrowed jacket around my shoulder,

I'm not frozen, but I feel so much colder.

I was never a guesser, I'm no guitarist,

But I can be your signboard leading you through the forest,

I don't wanna try modest,

So let's be honest.

I'm done pressing ice to my battle wounds,

I'm done piling blankets – it's gonna be May soon,

I'm done blowing dust on my piano,

Singing songs I wrote so long ago,

Words that should have been tomorrow,

Those dreams showed my glitters and forgot to come true.

Should I have picked on hints like I pick on my food?

Bite my nails down, let them bleed for good?

And if the knife was aimed at me,

How did it miss and end the story?

Now I'm in a pile of lost and found,

Waiting for you to come around,

Screaming your name – I was so loud,

But nobody can hear me now.

Dreamers with delusions, I'm no exception,

Trying to swim in an ocean, I tried every potion,

Just to make you look at me,

Once at least.

AWAY

Hold it before it goes like a bullet fired then regretted,

A dead man you once defended,

Catch it before it flows like water in a fisted hand,

Lost before it's planned.

Watch it scorched by the Sun, drowned by the sea,

Offending, the way it splashed so soundlessly,

Hear it before it is changed or spat like a smoking sash,

And all that's left is smoke and ash.

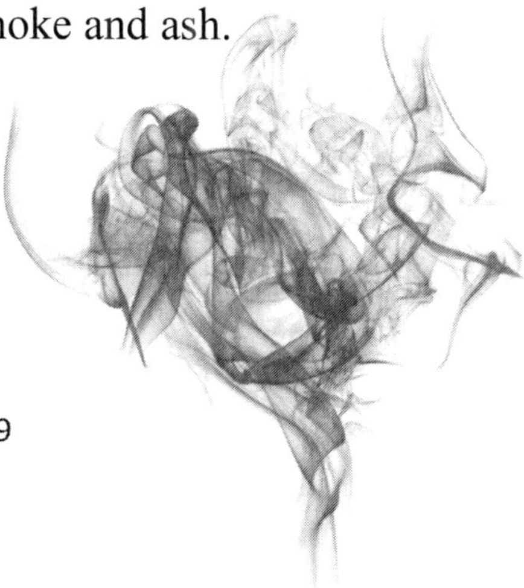

Maybe moments are to be lived in only when gone,

Memories changed only when they're disturbing or wrong,

Wars raged, and territories expanded when there's something on the other side of the wall,

Realization strikes late that you once had it all.

Your self-respect plummets like a marble dropped to the floor,

Shattered to a few hundred chess pieces or more,

And you don't know where you're heading or where you came from,

Every moment is like a shift for a new albatross:

Some to chain you to the ground or to teach you to fly,

Make your dreams real or make them all a lie,

Because even before Excalibur, you were something too,

A person you would do anything to go back to.

And you think the future is what you read,

By the lamplight right before bed,

Now all you see is a shadow, a scar,

An indelible mark.

Like a footprint in the mud,

Like a face drained of its blood,

Now you're living just to watch it return,

That what you thought would always be as it was.

Maybe it was a story you wrote all night long,

That lies crumpled in your dustbin like a melody you hoped would form a song,

Maybe it was a person you thought would stay,

Until you saw them walk away.

A MOON APART

A sliver of silver flash in my room,

I trace it like Ariadne's yarn in the gloom,

Touch it with bare fingers but they simply pass through,

Trying to find where it came from, hoping it's you.

It was hushed like a corridor holding its breath,

The darkness so deep - it looked like quick death,

And in the midst of it all this chaos it lay,

White like bones, bright like day.

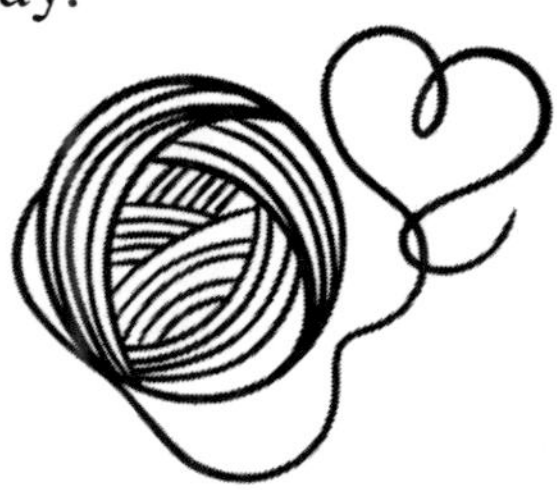

Glowing like a spirit, a candle in the night,

Full shiny armor, a warrior in fight,

Crescent like a watermelon I bit into,

The closer I look, the more it grew.

Like a deformed star on a throne of pixie dust,

Craters etched on it like a pizza crust,

I wonder if you are looking at it too,

As I imagine it carrying mail across the sky to you.

As the light streams in, it casts shadows on the walls,

Highlights my scars, for it knows them all,

If the sky were a tunnel, this was the light at its end,

A hope that makes me believe as it ascends.

It wades across the abyss overhead,

Making me wonder if it's all in my head,

When all is done, and all is said,

Will it still shine ahead?

I whisper words underneath its light,

My heart bleeds onto the paper till it feels just right,

And you'd never know it all to decode,

What I meant when I told.

I cried into the night, staring at the moon,

I'm stuck in this labyrinth, no way out, no time soon,

I try to climb the stairs it lays,

To castles and stars, where my boy, Peter Pan, stays.

Every drink of moonlight makes me fly,
Even if it is just in my mind,
It forms a hand, an invisible string,
Leading me headfirst, dreaming.

A sliver of silver flash in my room,
I trace it like Ariadne's yarn in the gloom,
Touch it with bare fingers, but they simply pass through,
Trying to find where it came from, hoping it's you,
Telling me my exile is over, the Minotaur's dead,
And the labyrinth I live in is just in my head.

HEARTSICK

It's not about being mad or storming out of rooms,

I've done both,

It's not about being paralyzed like a stag in front of a flashlight or howling like a wolf before the moon,

My coat of arms is now an arm of coats, if you know, you know.

It's not about mascara tears and battling fears,

Playing in the dirt, drawing stick figures,

I'm done with drama, I'm sick of karma,

Traveling around the world like Vasco Da Gamma.

I saw the stains on a silken cloth,
Made of starlight and intrusive thoughts,
Caught in a cage, caught off guard,
I'm not sick, I'm sick at heart.

The Pinterest sense of what the hell,
My chaotic thoughts burned into my flesh,
I knocked them down like a house of cards,
A domino array, I don't know where to start.

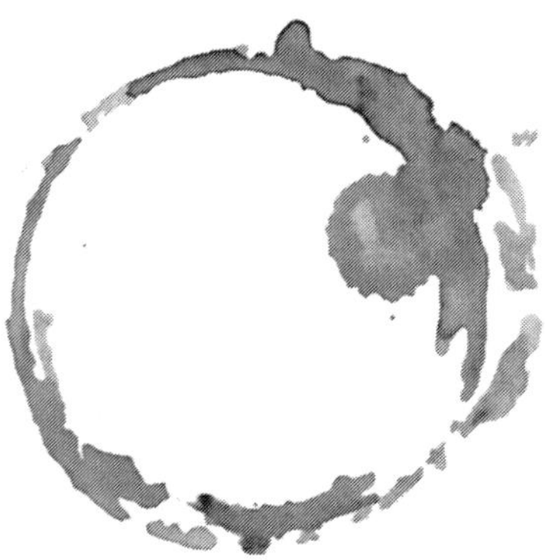

It's not about overthinking till all your wings are cut off,

It hurts and hurts till it's forgot,

I die from flaws in my own design,

I cry till everything feels alright.

I fake the smiles and stake the stars,

Break it once, break it twice, break it a thousand times apart,

An April fever, a winter weather,

A coat, a hat, a phoenix feather.

The sloshing sounds of a ship set sail,

The seizing nausea at a plan starting to fail,

The free fall before being caught by an invisible net,

The adrenaline, the pulse in my head.

I saw the stains on a silken cloth,

Made of starlight and intrusive thoughts,

Caught in a cage, caught off guard,

I'm not sick, I'm sick at heart.

The Pinterest sense of what the hell,

My chaotic thoughts burned into my flesh,

I knocked them down like a house of cards,

A domino array, I don’t know where to start.

I asked for a timeout ‘cause I need it now,

I dreaded it years ago, and I dread it more somehow,

Silver, sharp, a flash of a knife,

Time machines can’t put that right.

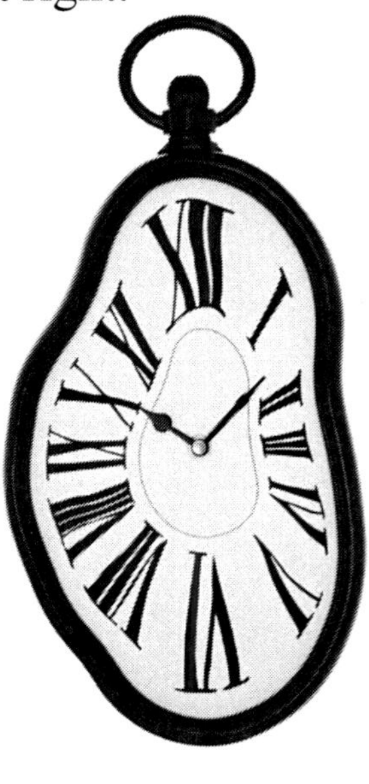

I read the stars to see if there was ever a change in mind,

I asked the doctor, he said I was fine,

There was no arrow, there was no scar,

But I’m not sick, I’m sick at heart.

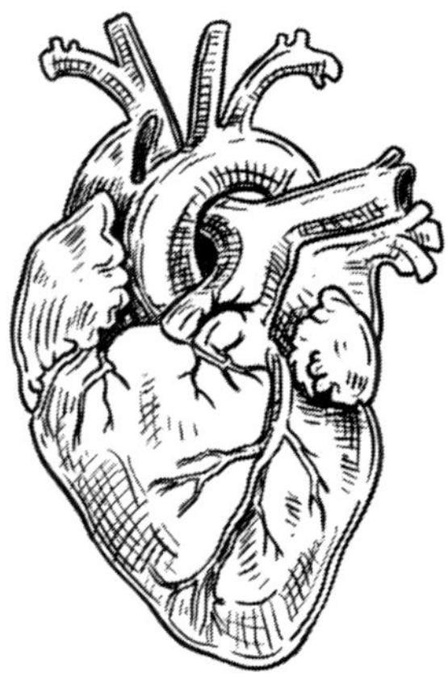

THE CASTLE I MADE YOU

Play-dough under my fingernails,

From building castles in the air,

Forced it through your mail,

Imagined your face when you find it there.

Oh God, I tried to keep the bricks from crumbling,

When you hit the final blow,

Oh God, I tried to keep it from falling,

But it would not hold.

‘Cause that’s the castle I made you,

I hate that I love you,

‘Cause that was the castle I made you,

I hate you, I hate you, I…

I can’t say it.

I tried to have it in all the colors we loved,

Purple blue November skies, yellow gold,

Pink sepia polaroids, gray secrets shoved,

Red from embarrassment, white-knuckled hold.

Oh God, I tried to stop them from fading,

To the blues and grays of my face,

Like a wash paint, everything is leaving,

Till there's literally no escape.

'Cause that's the castle I made you,

I hate that I love you,

'Cause that was the castle I made you,

I hate you, I hate you, I…

I can't say it.

I made the towers, the arches, the bridges,

I would've painted a sky of stars if you wanted,

I would've crawled through the hedges,

Of thorns and roses that once had me haunted.

Oh God, I tried to keep it from falling,

Into the moats I built around,

Drowning in a sea of tears - I'm not crying,

At least not for what you think it's about.

‘Cause this is the castle I made you,

I hate that I love you,

‘Cause that was the castle I made you,

And it drives me crazy 'cause I can't undo,

The fact that I love you, I love you, I love you.

P.S.

I built it for you, and now I can't tear it down.

NOSTALGIA

Nostalgia is a wave of energy,
Flashback to the old me,
It's like a bunch of wisteria blooms,
The scent of your old room.

Nostalgia is three dimensions,
New reality, but in my imagination,
Expanding till I hear, till I see, till I feel,
Everything like I'm there and it's real.

Nostalgia is being awoken by a bucket of cold water,

It's dreaming of happily ever afters,

It's the déjà vu of no returns,

Memories that make your heart burn.

Nostalgia is remembering the lyrics to your favorite song,

Thinking what you had was perfect all along,

Until you messed it up,

And ended up here.

Nostalgia is the salt tears on the pillowcase,

It's the sweet smile playing on your face,

It's like a rose - when it withered, I cried,

The moon phases - a change in tide,

Nostalgia is everything that leads back to that time,

Nostalgia is you and I.

THE SEVEN LETTERS I NEVER SENT

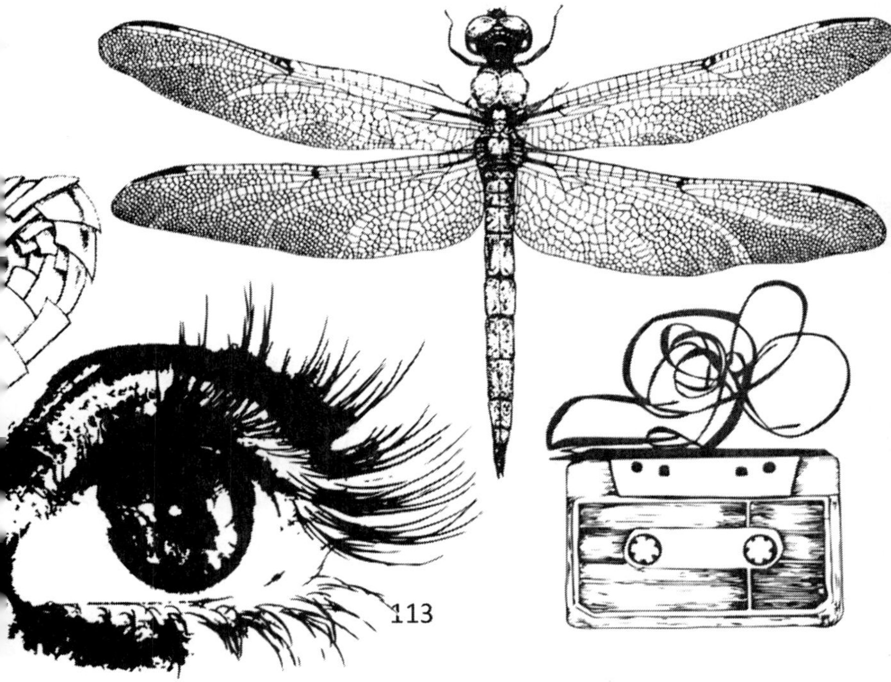

#1: I Care

Dear You,

Sometimes you know deep down that you could be everything for someone. But only if they let you in.

I care. You know that. You know that more than anyone else. Yet, you guard the door. Yet, you change the locks every single day. You build fortresses that no one can get past. All of that just to protect your heart.

I know it hurts, but it hurts me to see you shutting the world out while I'm still standing here, hoping you'll let me in.

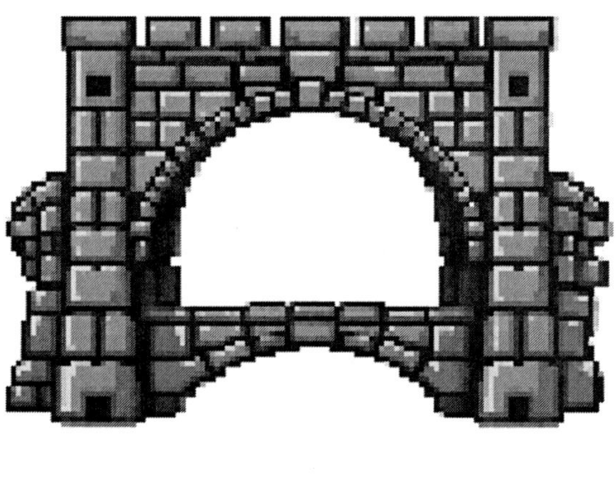

#2: The Forever That Ended

Dear You,

We filled notebooks writing forever, still spelled it wrong when it actually mattered. We prophesied this exact situation in a fight, and look where that's got us. We sealed ourselves in margins and pasted our fingers to walls with glue guns that shot webs of words.

And none of it matters anymore. Because it's all now a thing of the past. A fragment I cradle on midnights that have me staring at my own silhouette against my bedroom window, pen in hand, an empty page glaring back at me. It's a spell I keep returning to, almost a curse that keeps at my heels like a maniac monster who has nothing better to do. It's a time loop that would make Doctor Strange proud because the road ahead is endless and aimless, and the path behind is doom.

But all I know is that when we said "forever," we didn't determine an agreement period or an expiry date. We didn't count forever as a number of calendar days.

Then why do we do so now?

You talk of fine print and marginalia, the words unsaid that hang between the promises of two people too immature to decide, but I'm the one who reads and re-reads terms and conditions, I'm the girl who slips in secret details in them, but I'm not the one who gets fooled by them.

But you can't say that our friendship has run its course, like all the people before you who've told me the exact same words and have me thinking like all this is my fault. Because that's how you make me feel.

I once felt guilty for things I never did and regretted words I never said, but I know that even those couldn't change the outcome now, could they?

Just know I tried.

I really did.

#3: It Was Mine First

Dear You,

Of all the things that actually mattered to me, you chose this. I sought validation from it. I sought comfort from it. I sought the content that told me that I had it.

But then, you got it instead.

I had it for the longest amount of time. I wore it like one of my most precious jewels. They were proud of me.

What if they aren't anymore?

No one cares if it was mine first. No one cares about the amount of time I spent behind it. No one cares how much I longed for it. No one cares.

But I do.

It kills me, because it was mine first.

#4: Trying

Dear You,

I don't feel like myself anymore. I wear plastic smiles and rubber masks and control my facial muscles with the strings of a puppeteer, hoping no one will notice. I'm literally a ventriloquist dummy, and my brain is in control.

I laugh, but it's hollow.

I act like my life is this perfect thing.

It's not.

But I'm trying. To be perfect. To be brave. To be confident.

At least confident enough to look them in the eye without looking away, give a monologue without taking a shaky breath, and crack jokes without making them overly self-annihilating.

#5: Rendezvous?

Dear You,

No, I didn't expect to meet you,

But I love a good rendezvous,

If it's unexpectedly expected,

Leaves you shocked and then you're breathless,

I search for some evidence,

What is the chance?

What is the instance?

God, I love the circumstance.

#6: The Overachiever Diaries

Dear Diary,

What if I'm never enough for this world?

What if they think I'm too much?

They tell you to try harder the next time,

And then call you a "try-hard."

You chase the finish line with a shadow,

That pulls you back,

Telling you that no matter how far you run,

It will never be far enough.

I'm caught in the cobweb of this Paradox:

Expectations, contradictions – it just never ends.

The applause always comes late.

And sometimes it doesn't come at all.

Every success is followed by something,
That makes you cry yourself to sleep.
Every failure is a mirror,
You cannot look away from,
Until it's written all over your face.

And every victory hurts,
Every fall haunts,
But in the end the response doesn't matter,
You're still here,
Still fighting,
Still running,
Still trying,
To be enough.

#7: The Nostalgia

Dear You,

I miss the times when the biggest problem was how to become a class monitor or throw ninja stars at people you don't like (without getting caught, of course).

I miss doodling in the margins, writing silly poetry just so it rhymed, and being light-hearted about everything.

I miss answering every question, acing spelling bees, and knowing I'm not even in my double digits to worry about growing up.

And somewhere between missing those times and those versions of myself…

I miss you.

Dear Readers,

It's not The End yet. TRUST me, it's far from it. There are still so many letters I have stuffed in my diaries, hiding between lines, drafted in my inbox, stuck on a Word document, or locked on my Notes app.

I don't know if I'll ever send them.

But you *may* get to read them someday.

But this isn't the book for it.

To me, "Letters I Never Sent" is more of an innocent middle-school to high-school transition period where the hormones of adolescence kick in and amplify the smallest of details.

It's the feelings when someone else gets what you want, or those that arise when you're reading/listening/watching this romcom, that make you wanna scream in this high-pitched, excited way and then immediately call up everyone you know to tell them that your two favorite characters got together.

It's the anger, the hatred, the betrayal, the longing, the nostalgia, but at the same time, it's also the joy, the recklessness, the hope, and the love that always lasts.

So yes, there are some pretty strong feelings in here. There are some serious venting verses, crazy late-night musings, and over-the-top metaphors, but what's life without some dramatics and poetry?

I hope you enjoyed reading this book as much as I enjoyed picking poems and letters for it, because I really did. It was a rollercoaster of tears and laughter, eye rolls and "I should've known better," but here it is.

The 28 version of the Letters I Never Sent, dedicated to all those who've felt too much. To all the overthinkers. To all the delusional romantics. To the dreamers.

P.S: If you're someone I know and you think any of these poems are about you, they probably are. But on the bright side, I immortalized you in literature.

9 789356 023840

Printed at Repro India Ltd.